I0690952

Something About Grace

Bryan Joyner

PROLOGUE

The late-night sky seemed to hang lower to the ground than normal. It was heavy with stars and an endless sea of glittering lights that lit up a city that never quite slept. Grace sat on the balcony of the small apartment she shared with her mom with her knees pulled up to her chest and her arms wrapped tightly around them. The sound of distant traffic blended with the quiet whispers of life below. She loved this hour — the crossover into the full darkness of a summer night. Up here, she felt a world away from everything.

A cool breeze swept across her face and carried the faint scent of city life with it. It smelt of smoke, earth, hot dog water, and something else she couldn't quite put a finger on. She closed her eyes and leaned into the feeling of the night air against her skin as if it could wash away the weight that had settled deep inside her chest.

She sighed.

Grace opened her eyes and looked down at her phone, which was on the ledge beside her. No new messages. But it wasn't like she had expected any. She had learned not to expect too much from people — at least not anymore.

She reached for the notebook lying next to her and flipped it open. She ran her fingers over the worn pages that were filled with lyrics and unfinished songs. If she was perfectly honest with herself, they were more like half-formed thoughts. It had been her escape for as long as she could remember and the only place where her thoughts made sense. In this notebook, she could be anyone and say anything. She could write the words she was too afraid to speak and fully express her emotions.

But tonight, even the words wouldn't come.

With a frustrated sigh, she let the notebook fall closed and rested her chin on her knees. She stared out at the city and watched as the occasional car swept through the streets below. Every so often, headlights would find their mark dead-center in her eyes and cut through the darkness. Grace couldn't help but think that, somewhere out there, life was happening. People were laughing and falling in love; making mistakes and moving forward. She could see it all, but somehow, it felt like she was standing outside of it. Lately, she always felt like she was watching from a distance.

Grace stood up slowly and stepped onto the edge of the balcony. She leaned against the railing and felt the cool metal under her hands. The lights of the city blurred slightly as her eyes tired from the day. 'What's the word for it?' she thought as she scoured her mind for the shred of info she had seen on a random TikTok. 'Astigmatism!' Her thoughts were a muddied mess of random knowledge and the remnants of teen angst that were (supposedly) meant to be ebbing away now that she was officially a young adult.

Grace sighed again and this time was completely conscious of just how much she had been doing that lately.

She wasn't sure what she was waiting for or if she was waiting for anything at all. But something was coming. Something was about to change. She could feel it in the air — with the way the wind shifted and the night seemed to hold its breath.

But tonight, there was only silence.

Grace closed her eyes and let the quiet settle around her not knowing that it would be one of the last nights she'd have like this...before everything changed.

Table of Contents

Something About Grace

BRYAN JOYNER

Something About Grace

Chapter 1 –
Hairdryers & Flashbacks

The late afternoon sun found its way through the large front windows of Brooke's Salon in a manner that was so lazy you'd think that it hadn't even wanted to rise earlier that day. The scent of fresh shampoo and hair products filled the air and mixed in with the whirring sound of hooded hairdryers and conversations that no one in their right mind would have anywhere but a salon. Grace Moore was finishing up a blowout for one of her regular clients and her hands moved quickly but gently through the woman's thick hair.

"Looks like another masterpiece, Grace," her client said as she admired her own reflection.

Grace smiled and felt a bit shy as she held up the mirror for a back view.

"Thanks, Ms. Jones. You make it easy," Grace spoke with a voice that was soft and polite.

She had a warmth about her that the adult folk seemed to be drawn to. She had even been dubbed teacher's pet on more than one occasion. It was part of her charm, even though she didn't realize it.

Rene passed by with a playful smirk.

"I swear, Grace, you've got the magic touch. All the ladies want your chair."

Grace laughed lightly and tucked a loose strand of her own dark hair behind her ear.

"I'm just trying to keep up with you, bestie," she said.

Grace was only a few years out of high school, but she had already built a reputation for being talented with hair. She worked part-time at Brooke's Salon, one of the largest in town, while also attending Beacon Hall University. She had done a pretty good job of balancing her time between school and work, but she struggled to keep up for a little while when she took on a second job at Amor en la Cabina, the bar she worked at during the late shifts. The salon was her sanctuary, though, where she felt most herself.

The ring of the bell above the front door caught Grace's attention. A tall figure walked in and she took immediate notice of his stride, which was confident but relaxed. Grace looked up from her station and her eyes lingered as the young man walked in and scanned the room as if looking for something — or someone. He had a rugged but neat look — dark hair cut to a level one with a perfect fade and a casual jacket slung over his shoulder.

"That's Stefano," Rene whispered as she passed Grace after catching her staring. "Chris's cousin. He's here to pick up something for his niece."

9

Grace's heart skipped a beat at the mention of Chris, her high school crush. She had only ever seen Stefano in passing — usually at community events or when their paths briefly crossed in the neighborhood — but they had never actually spoken nor did she know his name. Now here he was, standing in the middle of the salon and looking both familiar and mysterious at the very same time.

Grace set down her tools and suddenly felt a bit flustered.

"I'll help him find it," she said quickly. But she said it more to herself than anyone else.

Rene raised an eyebrow and smirked again.

"Sure, you will," she teased.

Grace wiped her hands on a towel and made her way over to Stefano as she tried to calm the nervous flutter in her chest. He smiled when he saw her approach and she smiled back. But then her mind started playing games with her. She hoped her smile didn't look too forced. Then, she wondered if she had anything stuck in her teeth from lunch, so she quickly shut her lips into a politely pressed smile.

"Hi, I'm Grace. Can I help you with something?"

Stefano's smile widened as if he knew something that Grace didn't and caught her off guard.

"Yeah, I'm just picking up my niece's purse. She left it here earlier, apparently," Stefano said. His voice was smooth and so easy on the ears. It was like a sickly-sweet slathering of honey but in audio form.

"Uhm, yeah. That's right," Grace said as she nodded and led him toward the back where the forgotten items were usually stashed. "It's back here."

"Thank you," Stefano said as he followed Grace into the back. "She'd forget her head if it wasn't stuck on."

"No worries," Grace said as she shuffled around in the back. "She leaves things all the time, huh?"

Stefano chuckled softly.

"Yeah," he said but then he paused and added, "Actually, it's just what people say in these situations."

"Situations?" Grace asked.

But Stefano offered only a playful chuckle with no response. Grace couldn't help but notice the warmth in his voice when he talked about his niece. It made him seem even more likable. As she rummaged through the items, her curiosity got the better of her.

"So... you're Chris's cousin, right?"

Stefano leaned against the wall and crossed his arms.

"Yeah, that's right. You know Chris?"

Grace hesitated. She didn't want to dive too deeply into the old feelings she still hid deep inside of her.

"Uh, yeah. We went to school together. He graduated the year before me."

Stefano nodded and his eyes studied her for a moment.

"Yeah, I think I remember seeing you around. You were in the same year as Niko, right?"

The mention of Niko made Grace's stomach twist. She found the purse and handed it to Stefano with a smile. But her thoughts were already drifting into the past.

"Yeah, I knew Niko, too," she said. "Same year, different school."

"Oh, yeah. He transferred to Dunston for senior year," Stefano said.

"Yup," Grace replied nonchalantly.

Stefano took the purse and gave her a nod of thanks.

"Thanks for helping me out. Appreciate it."

"No problem," Grace said as she smiled a bit too brightly before reeling it back in.

There was a pause and Grace felt the air around them shift slightly. She opened her mouth to say something — anything to keep the conversation going — but Stefano beat her to it.

"So, uh, maybe I could give you my number?" he said.

This time, his voice was a bit more casual than before — more so than she expected.

Grace blinked. She was surprised but not totally put off by the idea. She felt a rush of warmth flood her cheeks and did her best to cool herself down.

"Yeah, sure. That sounds good."

"You alright?" Stefano said as he realized she was flushed.

"Yeah, uh, it's always so dang hot back there," Grace said as she motioned vaguely in the direction of the shelf she had just been rummaging through before pushing past Stefano as politely as she could. She needed to compose herself away from him if only for a second.

Stefano walked up behind her as she made her way to the front desk. He handed her his phone, and she quickly typed in her number. She tried her best to keep her hands steady. After she handed it back, they exchanged a few more polite words before Stefano left the salon.

Rene appeared almost immediately by her side and nudged Grace with her elbow.

"Well, look at you, Miss Smooth Operator," she said. "Listen, anytime a man's scent is left in the space he was just in, that's a win in my book. He smells GOOOD!"

Grace laughed and felt the butterflies swirling in her stomach.

"Rene!" Grace said in surprise.

"What?" Rene threw her hands up. "I'm just being honest."

"It's not like that," Grace said. "He just —"

"What?"

"He's just nice," Grace replied.

Rene gave her a knowing look.

"Mhm, sure. And you got all that from one interaction?"

"Yes," Grace said defiantly.

"You asked for his number, didn't you?" Rene prodded.

"Well, technically, he asked for mine," Grace said with a smile.

The two of them laughed, but just as soon as the laughter faded, Grace's mind drifted. It took her back to a memory she hadn't visited in a while.

It had been her senior year and Grace was all but swallowed whole by the excitement of prom. Back then, her world had felt small. It revolved around school, her friends, and the boy she had liked for what seemed like forever. Chris. He had been the star of the football team. He was athletic and popular, with long hair that always fell into his eyes in what just looked like the most effortless way.

Chris had been her friend first long before the crush ever developed. They had grown up in the same neighborhood and played in the streets with other kids. They had even walked to school together when they were younger. But by the time high school had come around, Grace had fallen hard for him. She just never let it show. When prom season rolled around, Grace had mustered up the courage to ask Chris to be her date. He had smiled at her and his easygoing nature made her feel like it had been the most natural question in the world.

"Of course, I'll take you," he had said as if it was no big deal.

Grace had been over the moon. She was convinced that prom would be her fairy tale night. But things started to unravel when Niko, the boy she had worked with on a science project, made his move. They had spent hours together in the library — hunched over textbooks and talking not just about chemistry but about music, life, and their hopes and dreams. Niko was smart and thoughtful. He was funny in a way that made Grace feel at ease. He had also been her friend when she needed one most. When her mother's business had taken a dive and they found themselves in a tiny apartment on the other side of town, she felt like her world was crumbling around her and taking her college aspirations along with it.

It was after one of their study sessions that Niko had asked her to prom — his prom, at a different school. "I'll cover everything," he had said. "Tickets, dress, limo — just say yes. And I'll come to yours too."

Grace had been flattered and completely torn between the boy she liked and the boy who had become a close friend. She took days to think about it and had even asked her mother for advice.

"Go with Chris," her mother had said simply as if the choice had been obvious.

So, Grace had told Niko she couldn't go with him to her own prom.

"We'll go to yours together," she had said — hoping to soften the rejection.

Niko had smiled, but it didn't reach his eyes. A few days later, he stopped showing up to their study sessions. Grace called and texted him, but eventually, his parents told her it was best if she didn't contact him again. Then, just days before her prom, Grace had called Chris to finalize their plans. He had been distant, distracted.

"Oh, right. I forgot about that," he had said casually. "I think I'm working that day, but maybe we can hang out next weekend?"

Grace had been crushed. She went to prom alone. Her dress and hair had been perfect, but her heart was so heavy with disappointment. The night had been a blur of forced smiles and awkward dances with a couple of girls from her class, but it was nothing like the magical evening she had envisioned.

Grace blinked and the memory faded as she stood in the middle of the salon. Stefano was different though. At least she hoped he would be. He seemed kind and grounded. Best of all, he was maybe even interested in her. But then again, so were Chris and Niko at one point.

Rene nudged her again and pulled her out of her thoughts.

"You okay?"

Grace smiled and shook off the lingering sadness from the flashback.

"Yeah, I'm good."

"You better be," Rene teased. "Because we've got a lot to talk about. Like what you're going to wear on your first date with Stefano."

Grace rolled her eyes, but her smile was genuine.

"Let's not get ahead of ourselves, okay?"

Rene grinned and tossed a towel onto the counter.

"Nuh-uh, girl. It's way too late for that."

But as much as she tried to hide it, Grace couldn't help but feel a flicker of hope. Maybe this time, things would be different. Maybe this time, she wouldn't be left behind. Maybe, she would finally be lucky in love.

Chapter 2 – Is There a Connection Here?

---

*T*he following week brought with it a rhythm that had become all too familiar to Grace. Between classes, her shifts at the salon, and the occasional late-night work at Amor en la Cabina, life seemed to be moving at its regular 50 beats per minute. But between all the hustle, Stefano had quietly slipped into her routine. It started with simple texts — a couple of questions about the salon here and casual comments about his niece there. Then, before she knew it, she was laughing at his jokes and checking her phone throughout the day to see if there was a text from him. It wasn't long before they started meeting outside of the salon and hanging out after her shifts.

Grace couldn't quite put her finger on it, but something about Stefano made her feel at ease. There was no pressure with him — no expectations. They just clicked in a way that was easy and uncomplicated.

One Friday evening, Grace found herself at Rita's Market, a small, cozy corner store that Stefano's grandmother owned. Rita Childs was a legend in their neighborhood. She was a woman known for her sharp wit and iron will. Despite being locked away in a state prison, her name carried meaning far beyond the bars that held her. Stefano rarely spoke about it, but everyone knew. Rita had lived a life that balanced on the edge of right and wrong. She used her street smarts to survive and thrive in ways that most people wouldn't dare.

Rita had allegedly run small-time schemes — dealing drugs and robbing those in the game — all while using her charm to open her market and cleaners downtown. The rumors surrounding her made her something of a myth. In the end, she was feared by some, but respected by most. Even behind bars, she still pulled strings. Her influence reached out through favors she could give or take away. For Stefano, his visits to see her were a mix of love, duty, and a deep sense of loyalty to a woman who, for all her flaws, had always looked out for her family.

The bell chimed softly as Grace pushed open the door to Rita's and the scent of fresh bread and warm spices hit her square between the eyes. It was inviting. Stefano was at the counter and as Grace walked up to it, she realized that he was leaning over to chat with a shopkeeper. They were completely unaware as they bustled around in the back. When Stefano saw Grace, his face lit up in a way that made her stomach flip.

"Hey," he said as he stood up straight. "You're just in time. We've got a fresh batch of cupcakes — your favorite, right?"

"One of," Grace chuckled.

"Well, I'll settle for one of," Stefano replied. "If you ask me, cupcakes are the answer to everything."

"Is that right?"

"Of course," Stefano joked as he finally walked around the counter to greet her. "Want one?"

"Yes, please," She grinned.

Rita's Market had been in the neighborhood for as long as Grace could remember. It was a staple, much like the Childs family itself. There was something comforting about just being there. The fact that she was getting all-access to the space made her visit all the more fun.

As they sat down by the small table near the window with cupcakes in hand, Grace couldn't help but feel the quiet pull between them. It wasn't romantic — at least, not yet — but there was something there. It was a connection she hadn't felt in a long time. If she was completely honest with herself, it was something she hadn't ever felt before. He felt like home and, yet, dangerously mysterious at the very same time. The easy flow of their conversations and the way Stefano made her laugh felt good.

"So, how's the salon treating you?" Stefano asked to break the comfortable silence.

"It's fine. Busy, as usual," Grace replied as she took a bite of her cupcake. "Brooke keeps hinting at something, though. I think she wants me to take on more responsibilities, but she hasn't said anything — like — straight up."

"More responsibilities, huh? Sounds like they're grooming you for something bigger," Stefano said with a wink.

"Ew, don't use that word," Grace grimaced as she bit down on her cupcake.

"What? Oh, grooming? Yeah, no. I get it," Stefano chortled nervously.

Grace shrugged.

"Maybe she is though. I mean, I love working there, but I've got school and the bar too. It's already a lot to juggle."

"You'd be great at it," Stefano said sincerely. "But I hear you. Don't let her overload you if you've already got enough on your plate."

Grace appreciated his support, but her mind was already wandering back to the salon. Brooke had been acting a bit strange lately. She had been dropping hints about "the future" and making vague comments about leadership. Grace wasn't sure what to make of it, but she couldn't help but feel that something big was coming.

As they finished their cupcakes, Stefano glanced at his phone and smiled.

"Hey, you free tonight? I was thinking we could catch a movie. You know, if you're not too busy."

Grace hesitated for a moment, but the thought of spending more time with Stefano felt right.

"Not one of your other girlfriends making you smile like that?" Grace teased.

"Other?" Stefano grinned. "Who's my first?"

Grace blushed and lowered her eyes. She stared down at the empty cupcake liner. She shifted some of the crumbs around with her index finger before folding it up and looking back up at Stefano with a pursed smile.

"I'm only playing," he said.

"I know," Grace replied.

"So, you game?"

"Yeah," Grace said. "Why not? I'd love to."

The next couple of hours went by in a blissful blur, starting with their walk to the cinema. Grace and Stefano chatted breezily and the cool night air carried the scent of street food and city life. They passed by lit-up shop windows and she just had to look at their reflections walking side by side each time. She didn't just feel at home with him — she looked it too.

When they arrived at the theater, Stefano held the door open for her and they stood for a moment in front of the movie posters. They debated which film to see for a good ten minutes before settling on a rom-com. It was just something fun to wind down the evening.

Inside the lobby, the smell of buttered popcorn hit them immediately. Grace looked up at Stefano as they approached the concessions stand.

"Popcorn?" he asked.

"With extra butter," Grace grinned at Stefano, who nodded in approval.

They added a box of candy each — Grace went for sour gummies while Stefano picked chocolate-covered almonds. Then they grabbed two sodas before heading to the theater. As they settled into their seats, the theater lights dimmed and Grace was surprised at how excited she was to actually be there. But it was about halfway through when their hands brushed against each other as they reached for the popcorn at the same time.

Grace felt a spark shoot up her arm and her heart skipped a beat. Stefano looked at her briefly, but when his eyes met hers for that moment, they both smiled awkwardly and pulled their hands back.

Later that evening, after the movie, Grace and Stefano strolled back toward her apartment.

As they reached her building, Stefano paused and turned to face her.

"Thanks for coming out tonight," he said softly.

"Thanks for inviting me," Grace replied as she tucked a strand of hair behind her ear. "It was fun."

There was a moment of quiet between them and the city sounds seemed almost muted by the distance.

"I'll see you around?"

"Sure," Grace beamed before heading in.

Stefano waited until she was inside and when she got up to her room, she looked down at the street below to watch him walk away.

The next morning at Rita's Market, the familiar ding of the bell above the door jingled as Grace made her way in. She had promised Stefano she would drop by to pick up some groceries for her mom, and she was looking forward to seeing him again. But when she stepped inside, it wasn't Stefano who caught her attention.

A tall, broad-shouldered guy stood by the counter with a tattoo that curled around his bicep and disappeared under his sleeve. His dark hair was tousled and there was something rough around the edges about him. He glanced up at her as she walked in.

"Hey," the guy said. "What can I get for you?"

His voice was low and smooth — easy like a Sunday morning as her mom would have said. Grace blinked and suddenly realized that she had been staring. She quickly stepped up to the counter and felt her cheeks go warm with embarrassment.

"Uh, just grabbing a few things for my mom."

The guy nodded and flashed a quick smile.

"Cool. Name's Dylan, by the way."

"Grace," she replied. "Nice to meet you."

As she rattled off her grocery list, Dylan moved with a surprising efficiency and tossed items into a bag with ease. Grace couldn't help but steal glances at him. There was something magnetic about him, like a charm that was hard to ignore.

"Hey, if it isn't amazing Grace," Stefano said as he walked up behind Grace and offered her a hug.

Dylan watched as the pair exchanged pleasantries. He was assessing the depth of their relationship and Grace could feel his eyes on her.

"You've met Dylan," Stefano said.

But his demeanor instantly shifted. Grace hadn't seen that particular look on his face before.

Grace nodded and pretended not to notice anything.

"You done, Dylan?" Stefano asked.

"Just about," he replied.

Stefano smiled through pursed lips at Grace as he waited for Dylan to bag the last couple of items.

"How much do I owe you?" Grace asked.

"Nothing," Stefano cut in. "I'll handle it. Let's get going."

Stefano was quick to grab the bag of groceries and see Grace out of the little store and Grace was left feeling totally out of place.

"You ok?" she asked as they made it out onto the sidewalk.

"Dylan's trouble," Stefano said casually. "He's been around forever. Knew him growing up. We live in the same building now. He's..."

"What?" Grace asked.

"He's not a great guy," Stefano said.

"Ok," Grace replied. "I believe you."

Her answer seemed to appease Stefano for the moment and Grace didn't think much of it. Still, there was something about Dylan that intrigued her. Grace left the store that morning feeling a little off-balance. Dylan drew her in. Maybe it was just curiosity, or maybe it was something more. Either way, she couldn't stop thinking about him.

By the time she got to the salon that day, things had shifted. Brooke had called a staff meeting for the afternoon and everyone was gathered around the large mirrors in the center of the room as they waited for her to speak. Grace stood beside Rene, feeling a bit uneasy.

"I've been thinking about making some changes," Brooke began. She scanned the room with her eyes. "The salon has been growing and I think it's time we brought in someone to help manage the day-to-day operations."

Grace had to stifle a side glance with Rene but her heart was racing. Her mind was mulling over a million and one possibilities and her nerves shifted from excitement to anxiety more times than she could count. But before Grace could process the thought, Brooke continued.

"I'd like you all to welcome Stacy Handswell," she said as she gestured toward the back of the room.

Grace turned and her eyes fell on a tall woman with sharp features and a no-nonsense air about her. Stacy walked forward and her heels clicked against the old linoleum floor.

"She'll be stepping in as the new salon manager," Brooke said with a smile. "I trust you'll all make her feel welcome. She's an old friend and her settling in here is important to me."

Grace felt relieved but it gave way to a bit of disappointment and confusion. She had thought Brooke might have been hinting at a promotion for her, but now Stacy was stepping into that role.

Rene nudged her lightly.

"You okay?" she asked.

Grace forced a smile.

"Yeah, I'm fine," she replied.

Chapter 3 –
Dreams at Amor en la Cabina

Grace tapped her foot nervously as she waited for Dylan outside *Amor en la Cabina*. After a week of casual conversations and texts, Grace had finally decided to invite Dylan to *Amor en la Cabina* for a special evening. Her favorite country artist, Anna Wilson, was performing that night. Grace had mentioned her love for Anna's music before, and tonight, the excitement was real. The evening air was cool and the faint breeze carried the scent of street food from a nearby vendor. She looked around and could feel both excitement and just a little bit of uncertainty bubbling up inside her. She'd only met Dylan once at Rita's Market, but there was an attraction there that she just couldn't get around. Stefano had warned her about Dylan, but she brushed it off. Stefano didn't know everything, after all.

"Hey," Dylan's voice cut through her thoughts as he approached her with a casual grin on his face. "Sorry I'm late."

Grace smiled and her nerves picked up a beat.

"No worries. I just got here," she lied.

Dylan reached out and opened the door for her and she blushed. He nodded for her to go in first.

"Well, since we were both late," he said as he walked in behind Grace. "Let's grab a drink and see where the night takes us."

The bar was crowded but it wasn't like it was out of the ordinary for a Friday night — especially considering the performance. It was filled with the sounds of laughter and music that spilled as sloppily around the room as the drinks that were being poured. Grace felt a wave of electricity run through her as they made their way to a small table near the back. She wasn't entirely sure what to expect from the night, but she was open to the unknown. For someone who always had to feel like she was in control, this was new for her.

"What are you drinking?" Dylan asked as he leaned in close so that she could hear him over the noise.

Grace thought for a moment.

"A mojito sounds good," Grace said. "Tell Danny to use the fresh lime, not that cordial stuff."

Dylan raised an eyebrow in approval and headed to the bar to order. Grace watched him go and drank in his easy confidence. He had this way about him that made him seem to know exactly where he was going no matter where he was. When he got back, he set her drink down on the table in front of her.

"Here you go," he said as he raised his own drink. "Cheers."

"Cheers," Grace replied as she clinked her glass with his.

As they settled into their cozy spot near the back, the lights dimmed and Anna Wilson took the stage. The room filled with her smooth, soulful voice and Grace was beside herself. She could hardly believe that earlier in the night, she'd been lucky enough to meet Anna in person backstage.

When Anna finished her song, Grace turned to Dylan with her eyes gleaming.

"Can you believe it? She actually offered me a chance to tour with her. All I have to do is record five songs. It feels surreal."

"That's huge, Grace. Just don't forget about me when you're famous, alright?"

Grace laughed and gave him a playful nudge.

"As if I could," she said.

As the DJ took over with louder music, Grace felt herself needing a quieter space to talk. She pointed toward the back hallway.

"Let's go somewhere less noisy," she said.

Dylan followed her as they slipped into the unisex bathroom. Grace didn't think much of it. It was just somewhere they could talk without shouting over the music. But when they stepped inside, Dylan leaned against the wall with a knowing smile.

"Didn't think you'd be inviting me into the bathroom on our first official night out," he teased.

Grace blushed and gave him a light smack on the shoulder.

"Oh, get over yourself. It's just quieter in here," she giggled.

"So, tell me about you," Grace said.

Dylan took a sip of his drink and a smirk formed on his lips.

"Where do you want me to start?" he said as he leaned back in his chair as if considering what to say next.

"What do you want me to know?" Grace shot back playfully.

"Ooh, ok. I like that. I guess you could say I grew up running around the neighborhood — getting into trouble here and there. You know, the usual stuff."

Grace raised an eyebrow.

"What kind of trouble?" she asked.

Dylan chuckled and looked around to see if anyone was listening.

"Alright, you asked for it," he said as he straightened up in his seat. "When I was about twelve, me and my buddies decided we'd start a 'business.'"

"A business?" Grace laughed. "What, like a lemonade stand?"

"Close," Dylan replied with a grin. "Except it wasn't lemonade. We'd go around the block with these cheap water balloons we bought in bulk and sell them to kids for twice the price. Made a killing that summer."

"Oh, wow," Grace said with a giggle. "An underground water balloon racket. Impressive."

"Hey, it paid for a lot of ice cream," Dylan said with a shrug. "But we didn't just stop there. One time, we dared each other to sneak into Mr. Holden's backyard pool."

"You broke into a pool?" Grace asked with wide eyes.

"Yeah," Dylan shook his head as he reminisced. "But we got caught by his wife halfway through. Mrs. Holden came out yelling and we scrambled so fast, you'd think we were running for our lives. My buddy Joey nearly tripped over the fence. I'm pretty sure I left a towel behind."

"Sounds like you were fearless," Grace smiled.

"Nah," Dylan said. "I just had a lot of energy. Didn't think much about consequences back then. Still don't, I guess."

He looked down at his drink and seemed to get lost in thought.

"I was never that brave. Or reckless," Grace said softly.

Dylan looked at her with a glint in his eye.

"Maybe you just haven't had the right kind of fun yet," he suggested.

"Oh, is that so?" Grace challenged his statement.

"Yeah," Dylan said. "Stick with me, kiddo, and you might learn a thing or two."

They laughed and as they continued talking, she shared more about her dreams of performing and her excitement for the future. She felt a wave of anticipation at the idea of all the possibilities. It was like her life was opening up in ways she hadn't expected. For a moment, she forgot the world outside.

Grace and Dylan stepped out of the bathroom — still talking and laughing. But they didn't see Stacy nearby. She watched them with her arms crossed and an eyebrow raised. A small smirk spread on her face as she watched. Then she turned and walked back into the crowd with a look that promised trouble.

Grace was none the wiser. When they made it back to their table, she laughed at Dylan's wild stories and was surprised at how different his world seemed from her own. He was rough around the edges, yes, but there was something charming about him.

"So, what do you think?" Dylan asked by the end of the night.

"About what?" Grace replied.

"About me," Dylan said as playfully framed his face.

"I think," Grace began as she sized him up, "you're interesting."

Dylan cocked his head back and let out a booming laugh.

"I'll take that," he said. "Could be worse."

They both laughed and the sound blended with the background noise of the bar. Grace felt herself relax even more and her initial nerves faded as she enjoyed the moment. The last hour of the evening went on like that: drinks, laughter, and a weird sense of comfort she hadn't expected. By the time they left the bar, she was glad that she had decided to go out with him.

But as they walked back, Grace kept hearing Stefano's words echoing in her mind.

Dylan's trouble.

She frowned and shook it off.

"You ok?" Dylan asked.

"Yeah. I just forgot something at work. It's nothing though."

The next day at the salon, Grace was working on a client's blowout when she heard the familiar chime of the doorbell. She looked up and her heart skipped a beat when she saw Stefano walking in. He looked around and his eyes landed on her with a mix of curiosity and something else she couldn't quite place.

"Hey, you're back already?" Grace asked, keeping her tone light as she finished up with her client.

Stefano shrugged and leaned against the wall near her station.

"Needed a haircut," he said as he assessed her face. "Thought I'd drop by and see my favorite stylist."

Grace rolled her eyes, but she couldn't help smiling.

"Nice try. You know I'm the only one here you know well enough to say that to."

"Fair enough," he laughed and crossed his arms as he watched her work.

When she finished with her client, she grabbed a broom and started sweeping up the hair on the floor. Stefano stayed where he was and watched her in silence for a moment before finally speaking up.

"So. I heard you went out with Dylan last night," he said.

His tone was casual, but Grace could sense the concern behind it. But she shrugged and tried to play it cool.

"Yeah, we had a good time, I guess," Grace said. "Why do you ask?"

Stefano sighed and ran a hand through his hair.

"Look, I know it's none of my business and we are just *friends*, but Dylan's not exactly the best choice."

Grace felt immediately defensive and she didn't even know why.

"And why's that?" she asked, but she kept her eyes down on the task in front of her.

"Just trust me on this one," Stefano said firmly. "He's got a lot going on. Stuff you don't want to get involved with."

Grace looked up and gave him a pointed look.

"And how would you know?" she asked.

"Because I grew up around him, Grace. I know him," Stefano replied in frustration. "I just don't want to see you get hurt."

Grace felt a mix of emotions from confusion to irritation and even a slight twinge of guilt. She appreciated Stefano's concern, but part of her felt like he was overstepping.

"I can take care of myself," she said. "I'm not a little kid, Stefano."

Stefano looked at her for a long moment before finally nodding.

"I just thought," he started up before his face hardened. "Fine. Just be careful, okay?"

"I will," Grace replied, but she could still feel the tension floating around between them.

Stefano sighed and looked down at the floor for a moment.

"Listen, Grace," he said finally. "I don't need to know about what you and Dylan do. That's your business."

Grace nodded, but she felt a little pang of something that she couldn't quite place. She tried her best not to let it show.

She was about to go back to her station when a petite girl sidled up next to her. It was Cali. She was new to the salon and Grace had tried to make her time there as laid back as possible. She knew what it was like to be the new girl, but what Cali said next threw her for a loop.

"Hey, Grace," the girl said softly and almost hesitantly as she brushed a loose curl away from her face. Her big, dark eyes sparkled with curiosity.

"Oh, hey," Grace replied with a welcoming nod. "What's up?"

Cali hesitated for a second as she looked quickly toward the door where Stefano had exited.

"Um... are you and Stefano, like, a thing? Because, if not, I was wondering if I could maybe... get his number?" she asked.

Grace raised an eyebrow. She was surprised by the question.

"Oh, no, we're just friends," she chuckled lightly. "Sure, I can connect you two. He's a good guy."

"Really?" Cali asked as her eyes lit up. "That would be awesome. Thanks, Grace."

Grace smiled and watched Cali walk back to her station. Her mind started registering the small favor she'd agreed to and she didn't understand why the thought of Stefano with Cali irritated her, but it kind of did. She couldn't help noticing how Cali's whole face had brightened at the thought of Stefano.

As the afternoon wore on, the salon got busier than normal and Grace found herself caught up in the rush of clients, appointments, and chatter. But she still felt uneasy about Stefano's words. She didn't want to admit it, but part of her was starting to wonder if there was more to Dylan than she had initially thought.

Stacy watched as Grace finished up with a client and her eyes narrowed in disapproval. Grace was skilled. There was no doubt, but lately, she'd been distracted — always sneaking glances at her phone or rushing to answer texts. She approached Brooke during a quiet moment in the back room.

"Hey, Brooke, got a minute?" Stacy asked casually.

"Of course," Brooke replied as she paused her inventory recording and looked up from her clipboard. "What's on your mind?"

Stacy leaned against the counter and chose her words carefully.

"Look, I know Grace is a good stylist. She's talented, but lately... I don't know. She's been slipping. Showing up late here and there and getting caught up with — well — let's just say distractions."

Brooke raised an eyebrow.

"Distractions?" she asked.

"Yeah," Stacy nodded and let out a sigh. "I think it's this new guy she's seeing. I just don't want her letting personal stuff get in the way of work. You know how important it is to keep this place running smoothly."

"I hadn't noticed, but I'll keep an eye on it. I don't want her going off track, either."

Stacy felt satisfied with herself.

"Exactly," she said. "Maybe a little talk would set her straight. Just a reminder to keep things professional."

"You think so?" Brooke asked.

"Yeah. I'd be happy to speak with her. Give her a little pep talk."

"Ok, *Manager*," Brooke smiled. "Take charge then."

At the end of the day, Grace found herself at the salon alone with Stacy as she finished cleaning her station. Stacy had been watching her closely all day and making subtle comments about her work as well as her interactions with clients. Grace tried to brush it off, but she couldn't ignore the irritation that was building.

"Grace," Stacy said suddenly as she broke the silence. "Mind if I give you a bit of advice?"

"Sure," Grace replied as she wrapped her duties.

"You've got potential. No doubt about it," Stacy began with her tone almost friendly. "But you've got to learn to stay focused. You can't let distractions get in the way."

Grace frowned.

"I'm not entirely sure where this is going. What do you mean?" she asked bluntly.

Stacy tilted her head and smiled.

"I've noticed you're close with some of the clients. And with certain visitors, too."

Grace felt her cheeks flush and realized that Stacy was talking about Stefano.

"He's just a friend," she said, trying to keep her voice steady.

"Friend or not, it's good to keep things professional in a professional space," Stacy replied smoothly. "This job takes focus. You can't afford to get sidetracked."

Grace nodded, but a part of her felt irritated by Stacy's words. She knew how to balance her work and her personal life — she didn't need someone else telling her what to do.

"Thanks for the advice," Grace said politely.

Stacy raised an eyebrow as if she sensed the resistance in Grace's voice.

"Just something to keep in mind," she said dismissively.

As Grace finished up and prepared to leave, she felt Stacy watching her every move. It was a strange, uncomfortable sensation, and she didn't like it one bit.

Over the next few days, the weird vibes with Stefano continued to linger. Their conversations became shorter and more strained. Grace found herself thinking about him more than she wanted to admit and wondered if she had made the right choice by going out with Dylan.

One evening, as she was leaving the bar after her shift, her phone buzzed with a text from Stefano.

Hope you're being careful. Just looking out for you.

Grace stared at the message with a waterfall of emotions crashing inside her. She appreciated Stefano's concern, but part of her resented him for making her out to seem like some type of little kid. She didn't want to be told what to do, especially when it came to her personal life.

I'm fine, she typed back, but she hesitated before hitting send.

"Am I being too hard on him?" she said aloud.

After a moment, she sighed and hit send before tucking her phone back into her pocket. She walked home with her thoughts heavier than ever before.

Chapter 4 –
Missteps & Consequences

G race stretched out on her bed and scrolled through her phone absentmindedly. She had been mindlessly scrolling through TikTok when her phone buzzed. She glanced at the screen and saw Dylan's name light up. Her thumb hovered over the notification before she opened it. She felt instant butterflies in her belly and she rolled over onto it as she propped herself up on her elbows. She clicked on it.

"I miss you," his text read.

She smiled at the message and buried her face in the comforter below her. What was she supposed to say to that? She missed him too, but she didn't want him thinking that he had her wrapped around his finger.

Dylan is typing...

"Come over to my place," the next text read.

Grace's brows shot up as she sat up straighter.

'Come over?' she thought.

It felt like a bold move considering they'd only hung out a few times. She stared at the message with her heart racing. Was it too soon? What did he really mean? She hesitated before typing back.

"Uhm, come over for???" she replied and bit her lip as she hit send.

The response came almost instantly.

"Relax. Just to watch a movie. Nothing else."

Grace exhaled and smiled a little. She could handle that. Movies were innocent. That was unless he was looking for a little Netflix and chill and this was his way of trying to get it. She felt nervous and didn't want to put him off, but she also didn't want to put herself in a situation that could turn ugly.

'I'm overthinking this,' Grace thought to herself.

"Okay," she typed back. After a moment's pause, she added, "What time?"

"Tomorrow night. 7?" he replied with a smiley emoji.

Dylan is typing...

"That work for you?"

"Yeah, I can make that work," Grace replied.

Her phone pinged again: a heart-eyed emoji.

Grace's nerves fluttered as she tossed her phone onto the bed. Tomorrow night felt so far away, but she was already wondering what kind of vibe she'd bring. Would she be laid-back

Grace or someone a little more polished? Should she take something with her — a pizza maybe or something to drink?

The next evening, Grace stood in front of her mirror and painstakingly analyzed her reflection. It wasn't because she wanted to impress him that badly but more because she was frozen in anxiety. She held up a lacy bra and matching panties she'd dug out of the back of her drawer.

"It's not going to go that far," she told herself. But her voice was quiet and uncertain. "But just in case he gets a peek..."

She trailed off and let out a nervous laugh. Her cheeks flushed as she imagined the possibility, but she brushed it aside just as quickly as it had popped into her head.

Sliding into the lingerie, she caught her reflection again and gave herself an approving nod. It wasn't about him anyway. She just wanted to feel as confident as she could. She rummaged through her closet and pulled out a fitted pair of jeans and a cropped sweater. It was casual but hugged her figure just enough. As she slipped on her jeans, she glanced at her small collection of perfumes.

'Which one?'

She picked up her go-to scent: Summer Girl. It was a sweet mix of vanilla and jasmine that always made her feel a little more alive. She gave her wrist a spritz and pressed it lightly against her neck to transfer the fragrance.

"Subtle, but memorable," she whispered with a grin.

Grace stood there for a good minute and took in her reflection one more time. She wondered whether she was making a big mistake, but she so desperately wanted it to be right. Dylan was amazing. He was everything she thought she wanted in a man and they had a genuine mental connection — not just a physical one. She knew how hard that was to come by these days.

Her phone buzzed on the nightstand and she grabbed it. It was Dylan.

"You still coming over?" his text asked.

It was followed by a pin location to his apartment. She clicked on it and the navigation window showed that it was actually just 15 minutes from her. It was already 6:40.

She quickly typed back, "Be there in 30."

Her palms were slightly damp as she hit send.

Grace grabbed her jacket and slipped into her sneakers before heading out. Her stomach flipped with nerves as her feet hit the sidewalk. It was still light out, but she ordered an Uber to help speed things up. There was one in the area, so she only had to wait about 5 minutes. But even that short wait was riddled with anxious excitement. The thought of the night ahead made her wonder just what kind of visit this would turn out to be.

The Uber eventually pulled up and she hopped in. She offered the driver a polite greeting and they were on their way. The drive was spent in silence as Grace checked her breath and made sure her pits weren't clamming up from the nervous energy running through her. She rubbed her palms against her jeans and fanned herself, but the driver spotted her movements and flicked the air conditioning on.

"Thank you," Grace said softly.

Soon, The Uber slowed to a stop outside a tall and old apartment building. Grace glanced up and took it all in. Her stomach fluttered again as she pulled out her phone to text Dylan.

"Here," she typed and her fingers trembled slightly as she hit send.

Her phone buzzed a moment later.

"I'll come get you," his reply read.

Grace slipped her phone back into her pocket and took a deep breath. She just wanted her nerves to settle down, but it was no use. Her heart was pounding in her chest and she could feel the thump of her pulse in her ears. The cool evening air did little to calm her racing thoughts as she shifted from one foot to the other and waited.

Through the glass doors, she saw movement. Dylan's figure came into view as he descended the stairs two at a time. She caught her breath as he pushed open the door and stepped out with a smile spreading across his face.

"You made it," he said warmly as he closed the distance between them and threw his arms around her.

Grace let herself melt into his arms as he wrapped them around her. His embrace was firm and comforting, and for a moment, she allowed herself to sink into the warmth of his presence. She smiled as she pulled back with her cheeks slightly flushed.

"Of course," she replied as she tried to sound casual, but her voice was softer than she intended.

"Come on," Dylan said as he motioned for her to follow through the doors that he held open for her.

The stairwell was quiet except for the echo of their footsteps as they climbed just two short flights, but for Grace, it felt like an eternity. She noticed the faint scent of fresh paint on the walls and the cool metal of the handrail under her fingers. Her mind raced with thoughts — how the night would go and what kind of person Dylan really was. This would be the moment to reveal something like that and even if he didn't intend for that to happen, his actions would tell her all that she needed to know about him and his intentions.

She looked at him as he walked slightly ahead and his easy confidence calmed her nerves just a little. He turned back and gave her a reassuring smile and her heart skipped a beat as faced forward again but reached his hand back for her to hold. She locked her fingers with his almost instinctively and by the time they reached his door, she wasn't sure if her stomach was flipping from climbing stairs or from the anticipation of what was to come. But when Dylan turned the key, pushed the door open, and motioned her inside, she took a deep breath. She stepped through and told herself to take it one step at a time.

Dylan's apartment was small but tidy, with a well-worn couch and a coffee table that was cluttered with random magazines and unopened mail. Grace stepped inside and looked around. She reminded herself to stay calm. This was just a movie night — nothing more, nothing less.

"Make yourself at home," Dylan said as he tossed his keys onto the table. "Want something to drink?"

"I'm good for now," Grace said as she sat down on the couch. She smoothed her hands over her jeans and pretended to focus on the TV.

Dylan joined her a moment later and sat close enough that their knees brushed. He handed her the remote.

"Your pick," he said as he repositioned himself to get comfy.

Grace hesitated.

"Oh no, you choose. I'll probably end up picking something weird and romantic."

"I like weird and romantic," he said with a playful smile.

Grace put her hands up over her cheeks and let out a playfully exasperated sigh.

Dylan laughed.

"Fine. I'll pick. But no judging my taste."

He grabbed the remote back and started flipping through options.

The comfortable silence was broken by the buzz of Dylan's phone on the table. He glanced at the screen and his brow furrowed for just a second before he picked it up and stood.

"Hang on," he said as he walked toward the kitchen.

Grace tried not to listen, but the apartment was small, and Dylan wasn't exactly whispering. She could only make out bits and pieces of what he was saying.

"I told you not now," he muttered. "Yeah, I'll figure it out."

When he returned, he looked like nothing had happened.

"Sorry about that," he said with an easy smile.

"Everything ok?" Grace asked hesitantly.

"Yeah," Dylan replied absentmindedly. "Ah, this is a good one: Strange Outsiders."

The night seemed to go off without a hitch from then on. Dylan made them some popcorn and Grace had even gotten comfortable enough to kick off her shoes and nuzzle into Dylan as the movie played. It felt like heaven on earth.

Then his phone buzzed again.

Dylan tried not to move too far off and turned the volume on his phone down before answering, but Grace heard the distinct sound of a woman's voice.

"I'm coming over," she said.

Dylan hung up and sighed.

"What's going on?" Grace asked as she sat upright and turned to look at Dylan.

"You know how it is — crazy ex drama. Don't worry about it, ok?" Dylan said as he pulled her back onto his chest before saying, "I was comfy and you've left a cold patch."

Grace grinned faintly, but an uneasiness settled in her chest. She brushed it off as the movie continued. Grace eventually put her arm around Dylan and let herself completely relax into him. There was no way something that felt this right could be wrong. She was just being anxious and paranoid.

'We all have crazy exes, right?' she asked herself in her mind. 'Plus, he smells so good.'

Then Dylan's phone buzzed again.

'You've got to be kidding me,' Grace thought.

He groaned and reached for it. As he looked at the screen, he stood up and said, "One sec."

This time, his voice was lower, but Grace caught the tension in his tone.

"You're where?" Dylan hissed. "Fine. Just wait."

When he came back, Grace frowned.

"Are you sure everything's ok? Is it safe for me to be here right now?"

"Yeah, it's nothing," Dylan said. "I just need to grab something real quick. Be right back."

Grace sat up as he walked to the door and a knot formed in her stomach.

Dylan paused and flashed her a quick grin before he opened the door.

"Don't stress. I'll handle it," he said.

Dylan unlocked the door, but before Grace could respond, the door swung open. A woman burst in, carrying two heavy grocery bags. Behind her, a little girl toddled in with a stuffed animal under her arm.

"Daddy!" the girl squealed as she dropped her toy and ran to Dylan.

Dylan picked her up without missing a beat.

"Gracie! Look at you."

'Daddy? Gracie?' Grace thought.

Grace froze and her mind raced as the woman stepped inside. Her expression shifted from annoyed to suspicious the moment she noticed Grace on the couch.

"Can I talk to you in the back?" the woman said. Her voice was sharp as she addressed Dylan but her eyes didn't leave Grace's for a second. Then, without waiting for a reply, she addressed Grace. "Who are you?"

Grace stammered, "I'm — uh — I'm Grace."

The woman's eyes narrowed.

"Who are you to **him**?" she asked.

Grace's cheeks burned. She looked at Dylan and silently pleaded for help. He stepped forward quickly as he shifted the little girl in his arms.

"She's my cousin," Dylan said casually. "She's been away at school. Just visiting."

The woman's gaze didn't waver.

"Cousin?" she repeated as her voice dripped with disbelief.

Grace nodded and felt her throat tighten.

"Yeah, I — I've been studying out of state. I don't come home much."

The woman's expression didn't soften.

"Uh-huh," she said as she crossed her arms. "Well, you can sit tight, cuz. Me and Dylan need to talk."

She stormed past them and headed into the kitchen with Dylan trailing behind her. Their voices quickly rose. They might have been muffled but they were unmistakably heated.

Grace sat stiffly on the couch and tried to block out the argument happening just a few feet away. She looked at the little girl, who was now playing with her stuffed animal on the floor. For a brief moment, Grace felt a pang of guilt. This wasn't what she had signed up for, but it wasn't the little girl's fault either.

The voices in the kitchen grew louder. Grace could hear the woman's anger. It was sharp and cutting, but her words were hard to make out. Dylan's tone was lower, but the frustration was clear. Grace wanted to leave, but her legs felt glued to the floor. She had no idea how to make an exit without causing more of a scene.

After what felt like an eternity, Dylan reappeared. He looked flustered but tried to play it cool.

"Mia's gonna drive you home," he said — avoiding Grace's eyes. "It's late, and I don't want you walking."

Grace blinked.

"What?" she asked.

"She's cool with it," Dylan said as he forced a grin. "Let's go."

The car ride was nothing short of excruciating. Mia kept glancing at Grace through the rearview mirror with her skepticism practically radiating off her. Grace sat rigid in the backseat next to the little girl called Gracie. She clutched her bag in her lap, while Dylan tapped away on his phone in the passenger seat.

"So," Mia said finally with an icy tone. "How exactly are you related to Dylan?"

Grace's phone buzzed in her hand. She glanced at the screen — it was a text from Dylan.

Say you're my cousin from my mother's side. Aunt Loretta's kid.

Grace swallowed hard and forced a smile. "I'm his cousin. Like I said. I'm Aunt Loretta's kid."

Mia raised an eyebrow but didn't respond. Then she said, "I thought Aunt Loretta's daughter was Tiffany," before going silent again.

Grace wondered if that really was the name of one of Dylan's cousins or another girl that he had had to hide from what was clearly his baby mama. The silence stretched. It was heavy and uncomfortable. Grace shifted in her seat and wished the ride would end already.

When they finally pulled up to her building, Grace muttered a quick "Thank you" and bolted out of the car. She didn't look back as she climbed the stairs to her apartment with her heart blaring in her chest. She felt tears welling up in her eyes as she got up to her room and looked out the window. Dylan was standing outside the car and smoking a cigarette — clearly a diversion so that he could look up at her. And he did look up.

"I'm sorry," he mouthed.

Grace drew the blinds and walked back to her bedroom door to shut it. The moment she closed the door behind her, she let out a shaky breath. Her phone buzzed again. It was another text from Dylan. She didn't even read it before deleting and blocking his number. Then she sank onto her bed and stared at the ceiling as the humiliation washed over her.

"What is wrong with me?" she whispered to herself. "Why didn't I just listen to Stefano?"

She felt foolish, angry, and — worst of all — disappointed in herself for ignoring all the red flags. But as the first wave of embarrassment faded, a bitter laugh escaped her lips. As stupid as it all was, it was kind of annoyingly funny. At least she was home. Safe. And, for now, alone.

Chapter 5 –
The Fall from Grace

S tefano adjusted his sunglasses as he walked into an unfamiliar backyard. The smell of good barbecue hit him right in the face and the sound of upbeat music set the vibe. The place was lively. There were kids running around and chasing each other while the grown folks sat at tables piled high with food. Cali had invited him earlier in the week and though he had hesitated at first, he figured it wouldn't hurt to show up. He spotted Cali and nodded to her.

"I'll be right with you. Help yourself," she mouthed and gestured to the food table before edging her way through people who were standing on the deck, and disappearing into the kitchen with a plate of hamburgers.

He grabbed a plate and loaded it with ribs, potato salad, and a slice of cornbread before finding a spot under the shade of a tree.

"Hey, Stefano, right?" a voice called out as he tucked into the food.

He turned to see a woman with sharp features and an air of authority. Her hair was slicked back neatly and her eyes scanned him like she was trying to size him up. He recognized her.

"Yeah," Stefano said cautiously as he stood to greet her.

"I'm Stacy," she said as she extended a hand. "Cali's aunt. I've heard a bit about you."

"Oh, nice to meet you," Stefano said as he shook her hand. "I didn't know Cali talked about me."

"She mentioned you a few times. Said you two have been hanging out."

Stacy gave him a smile but there was something in her tone that made him feel like this wasn't just a casual conversation. He motioned for her to sit and pulled out the chair across from him.

"So," she started as she leaned back slightly. "You're friends with Grace, too, right?"

The mention of Grace made Stefano pause mid-bite.

"Yeah," he said slowly. "We've been friends for a while."

Stacy's expression shifted slightly. From the looks of it, she became more serious.

"You seem like a good guy. So I'm gonna give you some advice. Keep your distance from her."

Stefano was totally caught off guard and nearly choked on his food.

"What? Why?" he asked when he finally managed to swallow the bite that had been caught in his mouth.

"Look, I don't know how close you two are," Stacy said as she crossed her arms, "but I've seen girls like her before. She plays innocent, but she's trouble. Mark my words."

"Trouble?" Stefano repeated with a frown. "What are you talking about?"

Stacy leaned forward slightly and lowered her voice.

"I saw her with Dylan at *Amor en la Cabina*. They came out of the bathroom together — looking all giggly and suspicious. It doesn't take a genius to figure out what that was about."

Stefano felt his stomach tighten. He didn't want to believe what Stacy was saying, but the image she painted matched his growing doubts about Grace's recent behavior.

"I'm not saying this to start drama," Stacy went on. "But you seem like a decent guy and I'd hate to see you get caught up in whatever mess she's in — especially if you're hanging out with my Cali."

Stefano nodded slowly, but he was completely unsure of what to say. Stacy gave him one last look before standing up and disappearing into the crowd. As he sat there, he kept replaying what she had just told him. He wanted to defend Grace, but a small part of him wondered if Stacy was right.

Later that evening, Grace sat on her bed and scrolled mindlessly through her phone. She'd been meaning to text Stefano for days, but every time she started typing, she stopped herself. Things had felt off between them lately and she wasn't sure how to fix it. To make matters worse, he had warned her about Dylan and she hadn't listened. She felt stupid, but she finally decided to bite the bullet.

Hey, you free to talk?

It didn't take long for his response to come through.

Yeah. What's up?

Grace hesitated for a moment before calling him. The line rang a few times before Stefano's voice came through.

"Hey."

But it wasn't an excited *'hey'* — hardly the greeting you'd give a friend you hadn't hung out with in a while.

"Hey," Grace said, trying to keep her tone light. "It's been a while. I feel like we haven't talked in forever."

"Yeah, I guess," Stefano said flatly.

Grace winced at the lack of enthusiasm in his voice.

"So, how's everything? How's Cali? I hear you guys have been hanging out a lot lately."

"She's good," Stefano said. "She's cool."

Grace's stomach twisted.

"Cool," she said — forcing a smile even though he couldn't see her. "So... I wanted to talk about Dylan. I know things have been weird lately, and I just wanted to tell you what happened."

Stefano was silent.

"I — uh — was at his place. Nothing weird or anything. Just to watch a movie and his baby mama came over with his child. Why didn't you tell me he was in a relationship and had a kid?"

"They're an 'on-again-off-again' type of couple. Besides, I told you he was bad news. That was on him for not telling you and on you for not trusting my word."

"I know —"

"Look," Stefano cut her off sharply. "I don't really want to hear about Dylan, okay? That's your bad decision, not mine."

Grace froze. She was stunned by his bluntness.

"Wow," she said after a moment. "I didn't realize you felt that way."

"Well, now you know," Stefano said frustratedly. "Honestly, Grace, you've been acting different lately. It's like you're not even the same person anymore."

Grace felt a lump form in her throat, but she refused to let herself cry. Instead, she tried to deflect.

"Oh, I see how it is," she said as her voice turned defensive. "Now that you have a new friend, you don't know me anymore."

"What are you talking about?" Stefano snapped.

"You and Cali," Grace shot back. "It's obvious you're spending all your time with her now. Maybe that's why you don't have time for me anymore."

"That's not what this is about," Stefano said with his voice rising. "But if you're so jealous, maybe you should take a look at yourself instead of blaming me."

"Jealous?!" Grace's voice cracked as her emotions spilled over. "You don't even sound like yourself right now, Stefano. I don't know who you've been talking to, but this isn't you."

"What about you?!" Stefano demanded. "You know, Stacy was right about you."

"Stacy?" Grace exploded. And that was all she needed to hear to open the floodgates — that someone she had trusted as much as Stefano had been discussing her behind her back, and with the new manager no less!

"You think you're so perfect, Stefano," Grace snapped. "But let's not forget who was there for you when nobody else was."

Stefano froze on the other end of the line and Grace felt her chest tighten. She knew exactly what she was doing — digging into old wounds.

"All those times you were upset about your family? About your grandma? Who listened? Me. I was the one who told you it would get better. And now you're throwing that back in my face? Just because you've got Cali now?"

"Grace," Stefano's voice was low. "Don't."

"No, let me finish!" Grace interrupted as her voice quaked with anger. "You used to tell me I was the only person who got you. The only one you could count on. And now you're acting like I'm some random girl you can just cut off because Stacy said so?"

"That's not fair," Stefano said. "You don't even know the whole story."

"I know enough!" Grace shouted.

There was silence.

"You know what?" she said when she was sure she was done. "Forget it. If you're so busy playing perfect with Cali, maybe we don't need to be friends anymore."

"Maybe we don't," Stefano shot back.

The line went dead and Grace stared at her phone with her hands trembling. For a moment, she felt a twisted sense of pride for standing her ground.

But the next day, Grace couldn't focus on anything. She kept replaying the conversation in her head, wishing she could take it back. By the time evening rolled around, she couldn't stand it anymore. She grabbed her phone and called Stefano again.

This time, he didn't answer.

Days went by and she tried again. Finally, he picked up on the third ring.

"What do you want?" he said.

"Look, I'm sorry," Grace blurted out. "I didn't mean what I said. I was just upset by what you said."

Stefano was silent for a moment before sighing.

"I appreciate the apology," he said. "But it's too late, Grace. Things are different now."

"What do you mean?" Grace asked as her voice began breaking. "We can fix this, can't we?"

"I don't think so," Stefano said. "I talked to Stacy, and... she made some good points. Maybe it's better if we're not friends anymore."

Grace felt her heart shatter.

"Stacy again? What did she say?"

"It doesn't matter," Stefano said. "I think she's right. This isn't working."

The call ended before Grace could respond. She stared at the screen with tears streaming down her face.

'Sometimes losing a friend who's still alive feels like a kind of death,' she thought.

It was a pain she hadn't expected and she knew she'd have to find a way to move forward without him.

Over the next couple of days, Grace confided in Rene. As it turned out, the news of her fallout with Stefano and the fact that Cali was actually Stacy's niece bubbled up to the surface. Grace could see that there was something more to Stacy's intentions, but the woman had done such a good job of painting Grace out to be some villainous jezebel that no one would believe her.

And as if she wasn't already dealing with enough, one next morning at the salon, Brooke gathered everyone for an announcement.

"I have some exciting news," she said with a bright smile. "I'll be opening a second salon on the other side of town. Since I'll be spending most of my time there, I'm putting someone else in charge here."

Grace felt a flicker of hope. Maybe this was her chance to step up and prove herself. Every time Brooke had talked about her dreams to open up a second spot, she had always hinted at Grace taking over the flagship — well, at least the daily operations, anyway. Maybe she would take her bestie, Stacy, with her and Grace could finally be rid of the disease that was Stacy.

"I've decided that, since Stacy has been doing such an amazing job in her new role, she'll be here full time. It'll be kind of more like a directorial role," Brooke continued as she smiled at Stacy.

Grace's heart sank. She glanced at Stacy, who stood smugly to the side and looked every bit the part of a new boss. Rene pulled Grace aside after the meeting.

"I thought that would've been you," Rene said. "Did you turn it down?"

Grace shook her head. She was too numb to speak.

"Stacy's been saying things about you," Rene added cautiously. "She's been calling you boy-crazy and saying you're angry because of what happened with Stefano. Do you think that's why Brooke didn't pick you?"

Grace didn't answer. She just nodded silently as everything crashed down on her. She wasn't even surprised that Stefano had been continuously talking to Stacy or that everyone else at the salon seemed to know about it. Her reputation, her friendships, and her job were all slipping out of her control.

"Rene?" Grace said as she looked at her friend.

"What's up, babe?" Rene asked.

"You don't think those things of me, do you?"

"Girl, I could never. You'll get through this, ok?"

"Ok," Grace replied as she choked back tears.

Chapter 6 –
The Stain

Grace stood at the bar of *Amor en la Cabina* and stared at the melting ice in her empty glass. She felt drained. Rene stood next to her and scrolled on her phone as she hummed along to the background music.

"You okay?" Rene asked as she nudged Grace.

Grace sighed. It was the kind of long, drawn-out sigh that seemed to carry the weight of an entire lifetime's worth of pain with it. Grace wanted to say 'no' — to say that she was God damn sick and tired of feeling anxious and out of touch. But, instead, she just said, "I guess. It's been a long week."

Before they could order another drink, Grace's supervisor — Trent — walked over. He looked at her and then at Rene.

"You look wiped out, Grace," he said.

"I'm ok," Grace replied as she stood up straight and made herself busy.

"That's not what I meant," Trent said as he realized she was likely feeling that he was scolding her for not being more lively behind the bar. "Why don't you take the night off — both of you? We're good on staff and finals are probably kicking your butt."

Grace blinked and thought, 'Yeah...*FINALS*.'

Again, she kept her thoughts to herself and just said, "You sure? I can stay."

"Go. Relax. You need it," Trent said as he waved her off.

"Guess it's meant to be. Let's go," Rene said with a devilish grin as she pulled Grace by the hand and led her out from behind the bar.

Grace shrugged and grabbed her bag as they walked out.

"You know what?" Rene said matter-of-factly. "We should get dressed up and go out. You need a girls' night."

"I'm so exhausted Nay," Grace said.

"Come on. You'll feel better."

Grace smiled faintly.

"Alright. Why not?" Grace said. "But can we stop at the 7-Eleven? I need to grab a box of tampons."

"You got it."

By the time they made it back to Grace's place, she was feeling a little more chipper. She stood in front of her closet and pulled out outfit after outfit. She tossed a skirt onto her bed and grabbed a pair of jeans. Nothing felt right. She wanted to look good but not like she was trying too hard.

She picked out a black top that hugged her waist and paired it with her favorite jeans. It was her staple when she wanted to do enough without doing too much.

"Ready?" Rene called out.

"Almost," Grace replied.

After a few moments, Grace walked out and said, "And?"

"Perfection," Rene replied.

"You sure you don't want to change? You can borrow something of mine if you don't want to drive to yours right now."

"I'm sure. Now let's go!" Rene said as she got up off the couch. "Tonight is going to be fun."

Grace nodded and let herself relax for the first time in days. They sang along to the music and recorded short videos of themselves laughing and dancing in their seats. Grace thought about posting it. She wanted someone to see her in a moment of happiness. Maybe Stefano. Maybe Dylan. Maybe even Stacy herself. She wanted to feel like she was on top of the world and give her haters a dose of FOMO.

'Later,' she thought.

When they arrived at the bar, Rene found a spot near the entrance. Grace headed straight to the bar.

Grace ordered her favorite drink, and as she waited, she looked around the room. Her eyes landed on a familiar face at the other end of the bar.

"Chris?" she muttered.

Chris saw her and waved. He walked over with a smile.

"Hey, Grace. Been a while."

"What are you doing here?" Grace asked.

"I came by the salon the other day to see you," Chris said. "I heard about you and Stefano. Thought I'd check in."

Grace frowned.

"You came to the salon?"

Chris chuckled.

"Yeah. Some older lady was locking up. She asked what I wanted... then started flirting with me. It was really weird actually."

Grace's jaw dropped.

"Wait, what? Who?" she asked.

"She said her name was Stacy," Chris said. "When I told her I was looking for you, she made a face like..."

"Like what?" Grace asked.

"I don't know. Like pissed off. I panicked and told her you were my girlfriend just to get her to stop."

"You said what!?" Grace asked as she covered her face and laughed.

Chris rubbed his neck awkwardly.

"Oh my God. Don't even sweat it. Stacy is ridiculous," Grace said with a smile but on the inside, she was seething at the thought of just how much influence Stacy was starting to have over her life.

"Yeah, she's... something," Chris laughed nervously.

Grace grabbed her drink and smiled at Chris.

"I'll — uh — see you around," he said.

"Yeah," Grace said as she turned to leave. But she stopped in her tracks and spun back around just slowly enough to prevent the drinks in her hand from spilling. "You here with somebody?"

"Nah," Chris replied. "You?"

"Just Rene," Grace replied. "You wanna come sit with us?"

"Yeah," Chris perked up and then cleared his throat to play it off. "I mean. Cool. Yes. I would like that. Let me grab a drink first."

"Ok. We're over there," Grace pointed to the table where Rene was sitting.

"Cool."

Grace walked over to Rene with a bemused look on her face.

"What was that about?" Rene asked.

"Stacy," Grace rolled her eyes. "She flirted with Chris and got mad when he said I was his girlfriend."

"His girl-*what* now?" Rene burst out laughing. "Oh, she's going to hate you even more now. That's hilarious."

Grace laughed too, but the thought of Stacy still ate at her.

The trio drank and danced the night away and by the end of the night, Grace was more than a little tipsy. Rene was still okay to drive after having decided that she would let this be Grace's night anyway. Rene and Chris helped Grace into the car and Rene drove them back to her place.

"I'll catch an Uber from here," Chris said when they made it to Rene's building.

"You sure. I have room," Rene said.

"I'm sure. Thank you anyway, though," Chris replied. "You girls get inside."

"Ahh," Grace fawned with one arm over Rene. "My boyfriend is leaving. He can't leave."

Chris just chuckled and watched as the pair headed inside. When they got upstairs, Grace collapsed onto the couch with her head spinning. Rene got a cold glass of water from the kitchen and placed it down next to Grace along with two Advil. Then, she checked that the door and all the windows were locked and shut.

"I do not need this girl falling out a window on my watch," Rene said to herself as she called it a night.

Grace eventually fell asleep and when she woke up a few hours later in the middle of the night, she was immediately hit with a sinking feeling in her stomach. She knew that she hadn't done anything out of the ordinary, but she couldn't shake this low, rumbling feeling of embarrassment and anxiety in the pits of her stomach. She could see the incoming streams of light from a streetlight outside. She sat up and rubbed her temples. Thoughts flooded her mind — her fallout with Stefano and Stacy's constant meddling. She spotted the water and Advil. The glass had already created a puddle beneath itself from the condensation. She looked around and realized that Rene had probably gone to bed.

Grace got up and gulped the pills down. Then she took her glass back to the kitchen and got herself a paper towel to soak up the water on the coffee table. When she was done, she sat back down on the couch and pulled the blanket up to her chin. She lay down for a moment and reached for her phone.

'Why am I feeling like this? What does that old hag want from me? And why does Stefano believe her over me?'

Grace shook her head and tried to push the thoughts away, but she felt a deep sense of inadequacy and loneliness creeping up on her. The more she scrolled through TikTok, the more videos that spoke to what she was going through that seemed to pop up. It was annoying. Grace quickly put her phone back down and it clattered across the coffee table. She stared up at the ceiling and begged her mind to focus on anything other than her thoughts.

She thought about the men that had been in her life lately. She had wanted to work out so badly with Dylan and despite the fact that he was clearly a low-life, she kind of regretted that they didn't get to take anything further. She knew that if she picked up the phone to text him right now, he would jump at the opportunity to sleep with her.

Maybe it would help. Maybe it would patch something inside her for a second.

'No,' Grace thought to herself. *'You're just being hormonal.'*

She picked up her phone again and checked her period tracker.

Period in 1 Day. Here's How You Might Be Feeling.

"I know how I'm feeling," Grace said under her breath and inadvertently dropped her phone back down without a hint of a clue as to how loud she was actually being.

Grace felt a tingling in her legs and knew that, without a doubt, she was feeling a little frisky because her period was on its way. But she just so desperately wanted a little bit of relief so that she could get some shut-eye.

She was certain that Rene was still fast asleep, so she placed a single hand between her legs and squeezed her thighs shut. She lay on her side, tucked her spine right up against the back of the couch, and began rubbing herself — first slowly and then a little faster. She fantasized about Dylan and then Stefano... and then both of them.

As Grace let herself get lost in the moment, Rene walked into the room. She had just hung up the phone with her boyfriend, who was worried when he got to _Amor_ and found that she wasn't there at the end of her usual shift. Rene had been heading to the kitchen for water, but she froze when she saw Grace.

Rene's eyes widened, and for a second, she didn't know what to do. Then, she giggled and pulled out her phone before hitting record. She tiptoed back to her bedroom and shut the door quietly behind her.

The next morning, Grace tried to shake off the awkwardness as she got ready for the day. She grabbed the tampons she'd bought the night before and realized too late that she had grabbed the wrong size. She groaned but decided it wasn't worth worrying about.

Rene drove her to school and teased her the entire way about how much she had drunk the night before. As Grace got out of the car, Rene called out, "You better Uber home! I need to get to class."

Grace laughed and waved her off before she walked into the building.

"Grace! I'm serious! You've got..." Rene trailed off. "She can't hear me. I'll text her when I park this thing."

Grace didn't notice the stares at first. But as she made her way down the hall, she began to hear whispers and giggles. She looked down and saw a dark red stain spreading on her pants.

Her heart sank.

Upstairs, a guy pulled out his phone and started recording her. Grace felt panic rising in her chest. Before she could react, Rene came sprinting down the hall. She smacked the phone out of the guy's hand.

"What is wrong with you?" she snapped.

Rene grabbed Grace's arm and pulled her into the nearest bathroom.

"Grace," she said with concern in her voice.

Grace looked at her and felt completely confused as well as humiliated. Rene explained what had happened and handed Grace her jacket to tie around her waist.

Together, they left the building and avoided eye contact with anyone on the way out.

Grace had gone home hours earlier. The house was quiet now. Rene sat on her bed with her phone in her hand and stared at the video she had recorded the night before. She thought she would show it to Grace later and they would laugh about it, but now she was wondering whether she had made the right call.

'Am I overthinking this?' she wondered.

Her thoughts spiraled and before she could second-guess herself again, she texted Janet.

"Can I come over? I need to talk."

Janet is typing...

"Sure. What's up? Everything okay?"

"I'll explain when I get there."

Janet's room smelled like vanilla candles and shea butter. It was cozy and calm. A muted TV show was playing on her laptop, which was open on her bed. Janet was curled up against her pillows and Rene sat across from her on a beanbag chair. Janet was the person Rene always turned to when things got complicated. She was calm, blunt, and never sugarcoated the truth.

"What's going on?" Janet asked as Rene sighed.

"It's about Grace."

Janet raised an eyebrow and brushed a strand of her curly hair behind her ear.

"What about her? You guys still cool?" she asked.

"Yeah, we're cool, but she's not herself. I don't know what to do."

Janet shifted and sat up.

"What do you mean? Like, what's going on with her?" she asked.

Rene chewed on her bottom lip and thought about what she would say next. She didn't want to sound like she was complaining about Grace, because she wasn't, but she didn't know how to be her friend at that moment.

"She's just... she's been stressed. Like, school, work, the salon, boys — it's all getting to her. And then there's this thing with Dylan."

"Dylan? Wait — who's Dylan?" Janet frowned.

"Some guy she started seeing," Rene explained. "Stefano warned her about him, but she's been into him anyway. And it's been messy. Really messy. I think it's over now. But I don't know."

"Messy how?"

"I don't know, she's just been all over the place lately, you know? Like she's holding onto everything and falling apart at the same time."

"Okay... and?" Janet asked.

Rene hesitated, then pulled up the video on her phone. She stared at it for a moment before turning the screen toward Janet.

Janet squinted, then frowned as she registered what she was looking at.

"Rene... what is this?"

"I caught her... like, you know... last night," Rene said quietly. "I didn't mean to record it to be mean or anything. I thought we'd laugh about it later. You know Grace — she'd probably make a joke and move on."

Janet stared at the video for another moment before Rene snatched her phone back.

"That's... not funny, Rene," Janet said. "Why did you record her at all? She's your friend."

Rene looked down at her lap with guilt written all over her face. "I don't know. It wasn't like I was trying to embarrass her. It just... happened. And she doesn't even know about it."

"Wait. Was that on TikTok?" Janet asked.

"Yeah," Rene winced. "I kinda posted it. I mean you can barely see her face."

"Why?"

"I don't know!" Rene got flustered.

Janet let out a slow breath and tried to choose her words carefully.

"First you need to take that down," she said before taking a beat. "So, what's going on with her now?"

"She's a mess, Janet," Rene admitted. "This morning, she went to school and… she had an accident. Like with her period. It was bad. She didn't even notice what was happening to her. People were staring and laughing. Some guy was even recording her. I had to run in there and get her out."

"She doesn't sound okay, Rene. She's going through something big, and you're in the middle of it," Janet said.

"I don't know if I should do something," Rene said. "I know she's going through a lot."

"What would you want someone to do for you if you were her?" Janet asked.

Rene thought about it and looked down at her phone with disappointment overcoming her.

Chapter 7 –
What's a Little Fight Between Friends?

N ot even a week later, Grace's videos went viral. Someone from the university had posted the video from the hallway and another user had found the clip of Grace from Rene's account. They combined the two and the internet exploded with comments and memes. It was the worst possible outcome and it had come true.

But Grace had thrown herself into finals and her music — virtually blocking out everything else, meaning it had been close to a week before she had checked her socials. But when she finally checked her phone, her heart sank.

Her name was everywhere.

"What the hell?" Grace whispered under her breath.

Her face flushed with embarrassment that quickly turned to blind rage when she saw whose handle had posted the first video.

"Nay?" she muttered. "Why?"

But before she could even think of a possible reason why her friend would do this to her, her phone slipped from her hands. She was shaking and she didn't think she'd be able to get it under control. Sadness swam through her and mixed in with the anger that was ebbing in her heart.

"I would never do this to you!" Grace yelled. "Why would you do this to me!?"

By the time her shift at *Amor en la Cabina* rolled around, she didn't think she'd be able to walk out her front door. The shame was so ripe that it felt like there were a million eyes on her back and she hadn't even made it down to the lobby yet. She thought of calling in sick but knew that there was a possibility that it would only make things worse. Her mom had always said that painful situations had to be handled like ripping a Band-Aid off, so that's exactly what she decided to do.

Grace's shift began like any other. She walked in and tied her apron as she tried to focus on her tasks. But the weight of everything — her reputation, the videos, the betrayal, and even Dylan — hung heavy over her. She tried to push the thoughts away as she wiped down tables.

That's when her manager approached and motioned her toward the back.

'What does he want?' she thought to herself and her face flushed for the millionth time that day as the thought of him seeing her in a compromising position popped into her head. She had been texting Rene all day, but she wasn't responding. All she got from her was: **"I deleted it. Someone must have downloaded it before I did and made this comp. I'm sorry."**

'*Sorry?*' Grace had thought to herself before she composed herself and bounded the corner to the back where the kegs were kept.

"Grace, Anna Wilson's team called," Grace's manager said as he handed her a piece of paper with a phone number scribbled on it.

Grace's heart jumped. Maybe this was good news. She really needed some good news right now.

"Thank you," Grace said as she took the paper.

"No worries," he replied. "Hey, you ok? You seem a little frazzled today."

"Yeah," Grace lied. "All good. Thanks again."

She quickly stepped outside and dialed the number. She couldn't help but pace as the line rang.

"This is Mark," a voice answered.

"Hi, this is Grace," she said as she did her best to keep her voice steady. "You called for me?"

"Yes, Grace," Mark replied with a clipped tone. "We've reviewed everything, and while you have talent, we have to rescind your participation in Anna's tour. There's an image issue here. Uhm, some videos."

"No, that's not me. I mean, it is me in the videos, but I didn't put those out there. I just —"

"Look, Miss Moore, Anna's brand is family-oriented and the videos circulating don't align with that. We simply can't associate with someone involved in... questionable content. Best of luck."

The line went dead before Grace could say another word. She stared at her phone and felt a cold knot twist in her stomach.

'How could this be happening?'

Grace shoved the phone into her pocket and stepped back inside. Her body felt like it was moving on autopilot. As she walked toward the bar, she froze. Stefano and Cali had just walked in.

Stefano didn't even look her way. He walked past her like she wasn't there with Cali chatting animatedly at his side. Grace's fists clenched at her sides and her emotions bubbled dangerously close to the surface.

Cali noticed her and stopped.

"Hey, Grace. You okay?" she asked.

Grace nodded stiffly.

"Are you and Rene good?" Cali asked. Her voice was light but curious. "I saw my Aunt Stacey talking to her the other day. She said Rene should maybe keep her distance from you. You know how my aunt is — always watching out for people."

"Why would you tell me that?" Grace asked bluntly.

"I just. I don't know. I thought you two were tight."

Grace stared at her blankly.

"Okay," she said flatly. Then, she turned and walked out of the restaurant without another word.

Grace had no idea what was happening. It felt like she was in some type of horror movie. Maybe this was some type of practical cosmic joke or something. Whatever it was, she was reeling.

The next day, Grace waited for the salon to clear out. She sat at one of the stations and stared at her reflection in the mirror. Her face was set and she looked like stone. Her darkened eyes just added to the seething feelings that were quietly brewing in her.

When Stacey came out of the backroom, Grace stood up.

"What do you want, Grace?" Stacey asked.

Grace took a step closer.

"Why are you always saying things about me? Why can't you just leave me alone?"

Stacey laughed dryly.

"Little girl, I'm only telling the truth. If it wasn't true, we'd have a problem, wouldn't we?"

Grace's hands curled into fists.

"You don't know me. You don't know anything about me."

Stacey shook her head and brushed past Grace.

"I know your type. You act all innocent, but you're just a corrupt little girl."

Something inside Grace snapped but Stacey was totally unaware as she turned her back to head into the backroom.

"Go home, Grace," Stacy called over her shoulder. "I need to lock up."

Grace's eyes darted toward Brooke's office, where the gun safe was kept. Grace was one of the only people who knew the combination to the safe and in that moment, she was glad she did. Her pulse pounded in her ears as she walked over and opened it.

By the time Stacey returned to the front, Grace was standing there with the gun in her hand.

Stacey froze.

"What are you doing?"

Grace's hand trembled slightly, but her voice was steady.

"Why? Why do you keep saying these things about me? Don't give me your bullshit answer of knowing my type. You've had it in for me since you got here, you jealous, old, has-been cow."

Stacey raised an eyebrow and called Grace's bluff.

"Because you're exactly who I said you were. And you know it."

Without thinking, Grace pulled the trigger. The sound was deafening and Stacey screamed. At that moment, Grace snapped back to reality and was instantly filled with regret.

'I've killed her,' Grace thought.

But she quickly saw that Stacy was clutching her foot as she collapsed onto the floor in pain. Blood seeped through her fingers and pooled on the tile.

'*Pft. She's not dead,*' Grace thought as her anger crept back in and removed any shrivel of regret that she had felt.

Grace stepped closer.

"Why? The truth," Grace said coldly.

Stacey looked up with her face twisted in pain.

"Because you remind me of me."

Grace stared at her for a long moment before lifting the gun and slapping Stacey across the face with it as she said, "I'm not you. You're not worth half of me."

Then she turned and walked out of the salon and left Stacey crying on the floor.

"Your turn, Nay," Grace said as she pocketed the gun and missioned for her ex-friend's house.

It was dark by the time Grace got there and she waited in the shadows until she was sure that everyone was asleep. When the last light went out, Grace crept through the quiet house. Her footsteps were soft on the hardwood floor. When she reached Rene's bedroom, she pushed the door open.

Rene stirred and blinked as the dim light from the hallway spilled into the room.

"Grace?" she asked.

Grace's face was streaked with tears but her expression was hard. She held the gun in her hand and pointed it at Rene.

"Why?" Grace asked, her voice trembling. "Why did you have to post those videos?"

Rene sat up with her eyes wide.

"Grace, I didn't mean—" Rene stammered.

"You ruined everything!" Grace shouted with tears streaming down her face. "Anna Wilson's tour is off. Everyone thinks I'm something I'm not, all because of you!"

"Grace, I wasn't thinking—" Rene's voice shook.

Grace stepped closer with the gun still trained on Rene.

"You weren't thinking? You destroyed me!" Grace yelled. "You've ruined my life. Now, I've shot Stacy, and—"

"Wait, Grace. You shot Stacy? You're not going to — I mean — we're friends," Rene rambled.

"A friend wouldn't do what you did," Grace blubbered through tears.

Before Rene could respond, her mother silently appeared in the doorway behind Grace. She was holding an iron frying pan and, with one swift motion, she brought it down on Grace's head.

Grace instantly lost consciousness and crumpled to the floor.

Grace's head pounded. She blinked against the bright light pouring into her eyes. Everything felt heavy and her arm was trapped under something cold. She tried to move but couldn't. She opened her eyes to the blinding light and slowly realized that she was in a hospital bed. She blinked down at her arm and saw that it was cuffed to the side of the hospital bed.

Her throat felt dry as she turned her head. A woman in a police uniform sat in the corner with a clipboard resting on her lap. She was chewing gum loudly and she stared at Grace with a flat expression.

Grace swallowed hard.

"What happened?"

"You don't remember?" the officer asked as she leaned forward.

Grace shook her head slowly. Her mind felt foggy.

Then there were flashes of Rene. The house. The gun. Her stomach turned.

"You pulled a stunt, that's what," the officer said. "Broke into a house. Pointed a gun at someone. Got yourself knocked out with a frying pan. And now, here you are."

Grace's chest tightened. Her voice came out in a shaky whisper.

"Where is Rene?"

"She's fine. Her mama is fine too." The officer tapped her pen against the clipboard. "But your salon manager? Stacy? She's one room over with a hole in her foot."

Grace closed her eyes. The memory of the salon came back. The gun. The anger. The sound of the shot. She felt the blood drain from her face.

"I didn't mean to—" Grace started.

"Didn't mean to what?" the officer cut her off. "Shoot someone? Scare the life out of your friend? You can explain that in court. It's out of my hands. You're going away for a while, missy."

Grace tugged at the cuff on her wrist. Her chest felt like it might burst.

"I didn't mean for this to happen," she said, her voice breaking.

The officer stood and stretched.

"Yeah, well, lucky for you, no one died. But the way things have blown up online? You've got people out there thinking you're dangerous."

Grace turned her head to the wall. Her body felt heavy. She could barely process the officer's words. Viral. The videos. Her mistakes were everywhere now.

The officer walked to the door.

"You'd better rest up. It's going to be a long ride from here."

"Can I see my mom?"

"Not yet."

Grace closed her eyes as tears slid down her cheeks. The room was quiet except for the sound of her own breathing.

Everything had spiraled out of control. Everything was gone. She quickly found out that her charges would likely be assault and attempted murder. The viral videos of her humiliation were shared alongside headlines about the shooting and the confrontation with Rene. People had connected the dots that the viral period girl with frisky hands was an attempted murderer.

Social media was relentless. Grace's name became synonymous with jealousy and scandal.

Soon, Grace was discharged into police custody and she did a painful walk of shame through the hospital to a squad car. Not far, her mother stood by with tears streaming down her face.

"I'm sorry," Grace mouthed to her.

"It's gonna be ok," her mother mouthed back.

That night, as Grace sat in her jail cell, she felt the shame of it all on 100. She was trapped, both literally and figuratively. She was imprisoned by her mistakes and the way the world now saw her.

Her fall from grace was complete.

Chapter 8 –
Locked Up

Grace sat on the thin mattress in her cell with her arms wrapped around her knees. The walls around her felt like they were closing in and for a moment, the cold metal bars looked like teeth in the dim light. She had never felt more alone. She thought about everything that she had gone through at the salon and all of the escapades with these men who seemed to just use her for a little while even though they had their own things going on the low.

She was angry. But above all else, she was hurting.

Her new cellmate, Clarita, sat on the opposite side of the room and watched her with calm eyes. Grace knew she was trying to get her attention, but she ignored the old woman and kept her back turned to her. She didn't want to talk. She didn't want to meet anyone. She just wanted out.

For days, she refused to speak. She barely ate and every time Clarita tried to say something, Grace would either turn away or pretend not to hear. But Clarita never pushed. She just went on about her day. Sometimes she would just hum a hymnal under her breath and fold her blanket neatly while she watched Grace. But she always kept to her side of the cell and kept all of her affairs in order.

Still, it didn't take long for Grace to realize how things worked in jail. The other women watched everything and she was pretty sure that they could smell weakness. They moved in packs. Some sat together at meals and some stood in corners. Grace tried to keep her head down, but that didn't work very well.

The first time someone reached for her tray at lunch, she yanked it back. The girl laughed and walked off. Grace didn't think much of it. She thought that was the end of it — like they were just testing to see if she had the guts to stand up for herself. The second time was dinner. A different woman walked up and stood in front of Grace. She didn't say anything. She just stared. Grace held on to her tray tighter and she felt her hands start to shake. The woman reached over and grabbed the bread, but Grace pulled the tray back and the bread fell to the floor. The woman looked at it, then looked at Grace.

"You're gonna get that pretty ass beat. You know that right?" the woman asked her.

Then she walked away.

Grace didn't want to show it, but she was terrified. Some of the women in there were at least a foot taller than her and had clearly been benching in the yard for quite some time.

Eventually, they started to slap Grace around a little at lunch and she had no choice but to give up her food on those days. Some days were better but by the end of the week, Grace was hungry. She sat at the table and stared at her food. She didn't touch it. She knew that they were just waiting for her to take that very first bite and she didn't want to fight. The third time, she didn't even try to stop them. She let them take the tray and kept her eyes down. She just sat there with an ache in her belly.

Breakfast. Lunch. Dinner. It was the same. Grace sat alone most of the time. Her body felt weak and her head hurt. She didn't want to ask for help or cry out in front of anyone. She just wanted to get through each day.

Clarita watched all of it and never said a word.

Then one afternoon, Grace snapped. When one of the tougher women reached for her tray, Grace shoved her hand away.

"Get your own food. What do you want — for me to die?" Grace demanded with hot tears in her eyes.

She didn't see the punch coming. The pain exploded in her jaw and made her head snap back. A second woman joined in and grabbed her from behind. Grace struggled, but she was overpowered. They kicked her and stomped her. In the end, they still took her food anyway. Grace could do nothing but just lay there with her face throbbing and her ribs aching. Two of the girls stuck around to finish the job and Grace could already taste blood in her mouth.

She groaned and rolled onto her side. Her eye was already swollen from the last beating. Now her lip was busted too. She reached for the table to pull herself up, but her arm shook too much.

A hand reached down to help her and when Grace looked up, she saw that it was Clarita. Grace's anger boiled over and she smacked the hand away hard before she pushed herself up without help.

"Get away from me," Grace hissed. "Nobody wanna help me. Just leave me alone."

Behind her, four women stood from nearby tables. Big women. Their eyes locked on Grace like they had been waiting for this moment, but Grace didn't see them. Clarita did. Clarita didn't flinch and didn't yell. She just raised one hand and the women sat back down at once. The room went quiet and calm. No one said a word.

Clarita turned to Grace.

"You done now?" she asked.

Grace didn't answer. Her chest heaved and her eyes were wild with anger as well as pain. Clarita pointed at the mess of food on the ground.

"You gotta get yourself another plate. No one will bother you."

Grace was too tired to argue. She got up and stumbled back to the cell before she sat down on her bunk. When Clarita came back later on, she watched Grace for a moment and then shook her head.

"You need to toughen up, niña. This place will eat you alive if you don't."

Grace gritted her teeth.

"Nobody cares about me," she repeated.

Clarita leaned back against the wall.

"That's a lie you tell yourself to stay angry. I care," she said.

"You don't even know me," Grace said as she turned away.

"I know more than you think," Clarita chuckled. "You ever been to Rita's Market?"

Grace frowned.

"Yeah. What about it?"

"I own it. And the cleaners next door. My grandsons are Christian and Stefano."

Grace froze and turned slowly. For a good minute, she just stared at Clarita in shock before she finally said, "You're... Ms. Rita's Market?"

Clarita nodded.

"Chris told me you'd be coming here. Asked me to look out for you."

Grace's chest tightened. Even after everything they had gone through, Chris had thought of her. He had cared enough to make sure she wasn't alone.

"Can I... can I hug you?" Grace stammered tearfully after a moment.

Clarita opened her arms and even though Grace hesitated for just a second, she got up and stepped forward. She let herself sink into the hug and felt the first real comfort she had felt in weeks.

"Could you have stepped in sooner?" Grace asked as she sobbed into Clarita's chest. "I'm pretty sure I'm gonna have a knot the size of a bowling ball on my head tomorrow."

"Girl, how many times have I tried talking to you?" Clarita chuckled.

"Okay," Grace said. "Fair enough."

Over the next three months, Clarita became more than just a cellmate. She became Grace's teacher. But Clarita didn't just teach her how to survive behind bars, she also taught her a lot about life. Who would have thought that a stint in the slammer was all it took to get her mindset right? Clarita talked. A lot. Grace didn't always want to hear it, but deep down, she knew that Clarita was right.

"Forgive them," Clarita said one night while braiding her own hair. "Not for them. For you."

"Why should I forgive anyone?" Grace asked. "They didn't forgive me."

Clarita didn't skip a beat.

"Holding onto anger will block your blessings," she said. "It keeps your heart too full of poison for anything good to get in."

Grace sat up on her bunk despite the fact that her eyes felt so heavy. The thought of showing the people who had done this to her any type of kindness made her inexplicably angry.

"What if I don't want to forgive?" she snapped.

Clarita smiled like she had heard that before.

"Then you'll stay trapped. You'll get out of this cell eventually, but up here," Clarita said as she tapped her own temple. "you'll still be in prison because you think the world did you wrong."

"But they did!" Grace yelled.

"Maybe they did," Clarita cut in. "But your anger won't change the past."

Grace wanted to yell at her and tell her she didn't know anything. But she didn't. She lay back down and stared at the ceiling. That night, she couldn't sleep. Her mind kept spinning with all of the rage and bitterness inside her. It was all she had been holding onto. But it wasn't helping her. It didn't bring her peace. It didn't fix anything. It just made her feel small and alone.

In the morning, Clarita handed her The Bible and Grace shook her head.

"I'm not reading that," Grace scoffed.

Clarita didn't argue. She just placed it on Grace's bunk and walked away. Days passed and Grace still ignored the book. But each night, Clarita spoke about grace and forgiveness. She spoke about the relief of letting go.

Grace didn't respond. But she listened.

Then one afternoon, a guard came to their cell.

"Letter for Grace," he said.

She took it and sat on her bunk. The envelope felt heavy in her hand and her name was written in bold letters. She knew the handwriting.

It was Rene.

Her first thought was to rip it up. Her second thought was to throw it away. But her fingers didn't move. Her eyes stayed locked on the paper. Clarita sat on her bunk and watched her, but didn't say a word.

After a while, Grace opened it. Her hands shook as she pulled out the letter and she scanned the first few lines. She didn't know what to expect. An apology? A warning? Another betrayal?

Grace,

I don't know if you'll even read this, but I hope you do. I was mad when you pulled that gun on me. I was mad for a whole day. But after that, I started thinking about everything that happened. I started feeling guilty. I should've never posted that video. I should've never let things go that far. And I should've fought harder to make it right.

I've been working with your mom to get you out. She's been doing everything she can. Stacey won't drop the charges, though. She keeps calling you a monster. But we got you a lawyer. He says because you only shot her in the foot, it can't count as attempted murder. He's trying to get your sentence reduced. Maybe even just time served. I just want you to know I'm sorry.

We're fighting out here for you and we'll keep fighting.

Rene

Grace read it twice and didn't know how to feel. She had spent so much time hating Rene and blaming her for everything. But now... now she just felt tired.

"Why wouldn't my mom tell me?" she whispered.

"Maybe she knew you'd recoil at the idea of Rene helping you. Maybe she wanted Rene to tell you herself," Clarita chimed in.

Grace folded the letter and sighed.

"I just don't understand why Stacey hates me so much?"

Clarita watched her carefully before she said, "Maybe because she sees something in you that she doesn't like about herself. People who hold onto hate do it because they can't stand their own reflection."

Grace thought about that.

"Do you think God thinks I'm a monster?" she asked after a while.

"No, baby," Clarita said gently. "God doesn't see you the way people do. People always get it wrong. God sees everything. He knows what's just."

"How do you know so much about God?" Grace asked. "I mean, you had a wild past. No offense or anything."

"None taken," Clarita laughed. "Actually, I wasn't supposed to make it this far. I made mistakes. Did things I shouldn't have. But God gave me grace. That's why I'm here. Why I have a family. A business. Safety."

"Grace, huh?" Grace looked down at her hands and chuckled.

"That's why," Clarita said as she leaned in closer, "you need to forgive. You've been given grace too. It's time you start living like it."

Grace felt a loosening happen in her chest for the first time since she had walked into that very cell. There was a lightness to it. Even though she wasn't free yet, for the first time in a long time, she wanted to be.

Chapter 9 –
Redemption

Grace sat on the edge of her bunk with her knees pulled to her chest. The cell felt colder than usual and her fingers fidgeted with the corner of the thin sheet on her bed. She had never really gotten used to that weird papery feeling of it. Clarita looked at her as she sat still in thought.

"They said it's set," Grace said. "Three days from now."

Clarita didn't say anything right away. She had been folding a worn washcloth and placed it down carefully before she looked over Grace.

"You ready?" she asked.

"I don't know."

This should have been a moment of relief for Grace. She had been in limbo for so long, but the idea of going to trial for attempted murder was anything but relieving. This could be it. Her life done and down the tubes. The thought of having to spend what everyone said were your best years behind bars made her feel queasy.

Clarita leaned back against the wall.

"What if..." Grace trailed off.

"You don't have to know what happens next. You just need to walk in with your head up."

"But what if they give me years, Clarita?" Grace's voice quaked.

"Then you do the time," Clarita said. "But you don't let the time do you."

Grace looked up and for the first time, the acceptance of possibly doing hard time washed over her. She couldn't fix this one, nor could she control the outcome. All she had to do was wait for her fate. Still, there was something weirdly freeing in that. When you can't control anything, what do you really have to worry about?

Clarita kept going as Grace's thoughts gave way to stillness.

"You've already changed in here. You might not see it, but I do. You used to wake up angry. You used to fight everything and everyone. Now you listen. You write and you think before you speak."

"Still doesn't change the fact that I shot somebody though," Grace laughed dryly.

"And you owned it," Clarita said as she pointed a finger at her. "That's more than most can say."

"I know. I just keep replaying everything. Over and over. If I hadn't gone to Dylan's... If I hadn't trusted Rene... If I hadn't—"

Clarita cut her off.

"Enough. You can dig in the dirt forever. It won't bring back the seed. What matters is what you plant now."

"But I'm scared," Grace sighed.

"And you're allowed to be, honey," Clarita replied.

There was silence for a while as Grace looked up at the ceiling to try and hide the fact that her eyes stung with fresh tears.

"Do you think they'll be there?" she finally asked. "My mom... Rene?"

"I know they will," Clarita nodded. "Your mom at least. I mean she has been here for every visitation possible."

Grace didn't say anything more. She just sat there and stared at her shoes. Clarita got up and placed a hand on Grace's shoulder.

"No matter what that judge says, you already started your healing. That's what matters."

Grace nodded and for the first time in a long time, she believed it.

In a matter of days, Grace sat in the courtroom in her khaki jumpsuit. Her wrists were cold inside the cuffs and her ankles too. It was the first time in nine months she had seen her mom in person without a sheet of glass between them. It was the first time she had seen Rene too. They were seated on a bench behind her, right beside her lawyer. Grace didn't turn around, but she felt them there.

The judge looked down at the file and then back at Grace.

"You've been here a while," the judge said. "Nine months. That's a long time for someone with no prior charges."

Grace offered a forced smile but stayed quiet as she could feel her heartbeat in her ears. Her lawyer stood up beside her.

"The charge of attempted murder has been dropped," the judge continued. "There is no clear evidence that you intended to kill anyone. One of the victims even submitted a letter to the court asking for leniency."

Grace's head lifted slightly and immediately knew that it was Rene. She looked back at her old friend who smiled apologetically back at her.

The judge set the file aside.

"Normally, this court would hand down the maximum sentence possible to send a message. We need to hold people accountable for violent acts, but this is an unusual case. And I feel that the consequences have already been felt."

Grace stared at the floor and didn't know if she should feel hopeful.

"I'm sentencing you to one year," the judge said and Grace's heart sank. But then she perked back up as she realized just how lenient that was. Then the judge said something she hadn't expected at all, "With time served. And two years' probation."

Grace let out a breath she didn't know she was holding. Her shoulders dropped and her hands still shook in the cuffs. She didn't cry. She just nodded.

'Three months to go,' Grace thought to herself.

And just like that, three months later, the prison gate opened. Grace stepped out of the gates with the morning sun in her eyes and she blinked against the light. It felt strange and the air smelled different. It was nothing like the scent of bleach and sweat and steel that she had become so accustomed to. It smelled like grass and fried food and exhaust. It smelled like freedom.

Rene waited in a small red car parked across the road and when Grace spotted her, her knees almost buckled. Rene waved. Grace walked slowly and then faster. She didn't even stop when she reached the curb. Rene opened the door and Grace fell into her arms.

"Hey," Rene said.

"Hey," Grace said.

Neither of them cried. They just held each other.

"Let's go home," Rene said. "Your mom's waiting."

They didn't talk much on the drive. The car felt warm and the music was soft. Grace stared out the window and the world looked the same but she didn't feel the same.

"We'll catch up when you're ready," Rene said as she pulled up to the house.

"Yeah," Grace replied with a smile. "And thank you for the letter."

"Hey, I kinda got you into that mess," Rene replied.

Just then, Grace's mom ran out the front door and Grace jumped out of the passenger's side. They met on the lawn and hugged for the longest time as Rene pulled back onto the road slowly.

"We have a lot to talk about," Grace's mom said.

"We do," Grace said.

The house hadn't changed much. There was still the same furniture and smell. To be honest, Grace didn't know what she expected to be different. It had only been a year. Still, she walked through it slowly like a guest. Her room had been kept neat and her bed was made. A Bible rested on her pillow and she breathed a heavy sigh of relief as she sat down.

Later that night, Grace sat on the half-window ledge of her bedroom with one leg curled under her and the other swinging slowly as she looked out at the city skyline in the distance. She wore a clean pair of soft grey sweats and an old oversized tee with a faded logo from a music camp she'd gone to when she was fifteen. Her feet were bare and her hair was tied in a loose bun that kept falling out. The late summer air drifted in and she could hear the sound of traffic and laughter from the corner shop down below. She closed her eyes and let it wrap around her.

Her mom had made her favorite that night — baked mac and cheese with garlic bread and spicy chicken fried steak. She had eaten every bite slowly and tried not to cry between mouthfuls. It wasn't just the taste. It was the fact that someone made it for her and that someone thought about what she liked and took the time to give her comfort. It hadn't felt like home until that first bite.

Now, full and quiet, she sat in her usual spot on the ledge. She hadn't realized how much she missed it. She decided to write and the pen moved in her hand without much thought. The notebook rested on her thigh as she looked down at the pages, which were already messy from earlier scrawls and scratched-out verses. She hummed softly and tested the melody that had been playing in her head all week. Her voice was low and steady. She didn't sing for anyone. Not this time. She sang because it helped her breathe.

The moonlight spilled across the paper as she wrote and her fingers smudged the ink slightly as she went. Then she paused and let the melody land and when it did, the lyrics came.

"Grace"

I'm not the girl they said I was

Not the name they tossed in flame

I wore their words like second skin

But I've stopped playing that game

They called me wild

They called me fake

But I won't bend, I will not break

I've made mistakes I won't defend

But I'm not finished, this ain't the end

I've walked through fire

Felt the shame

But still, I rise

Still, I claim my name

So call me broken

Call me wrong

But I've been quiet for too long

Now I sing

Now I write

And I am done with hiding light

My name is Grace

And I still stand

Not perfect

But I know who I am.

She looked down at the words and took a breath. Then she closed the book, leaned her head against the frame, and let the breeze wash over her skin as she sunk into the comfort of her freedom. She wasn't sure what was next for her, but she was just appreciative of the second shot at life.

The next morning, Grace decided to walk into the city. The sun was soft but warm on her skin. She closed her eyes for a second and let it rest on her face. It was the first time in almost a year that she could walk more than six by eight feet without a wall blocking her. Her legs stretched out longer now and her arms swung free at her sides. Each step on the cracked sidewalk felt like something she'd never done before. It was almost like something that had been borrowed from someone else's life.

She passed a mother holding her toddler's hand and a boy flying by on a rusted bike. There was a man whistling from his stoop with a toothpick between his teeth who smiled down at Grace. The street smelled like detergent from someone doing laundry and meat on a far-off grill. Grace breathed in and felt her ribs lift.

As she got to Rita's Market, the bell on the door jingled. The same old lady at the counter smiled and Grace was happy to see that there was no Dylan in sight.

"You're back," the lady said.

"Just visiting," Grace said.

She grabbed a box of her favorite kind of cupcakes with the buttercream swirl and the little chocolate star on top.

"Put it on Clarita's tab," Grace said. "She said I could get a box on her."

"Already done," the lady said.

Grace sat on the curb outside and opened the box. She ate one slowly and then another. She didn't even care if it got on her fingers. She hadn't tasted something this sweet in months. But as she ate blissfully, a shadow passed in front of her and she looked up.

Stefano stood there with his hands in his pockets. He looked older but not in a tired way. It was more like in the way someone does when they've been through stuff and come out the other side.

"Mind if I sit?" he asked.

"Public curb," Grace smiled.

He sat beside her but left space between them.

"You look good," Stefano said.

"Yeah. It's that 'just out of jail' haute couture. Thanks," Grace said.

They both laughed and there was a pause before Grace picked at the edge of the box.

"How's Cali?" she asked without looking at him.

Stefano shook his head.

"Nah. She was too childish. Always needed attention. Always caught up in some drama that didn't matter. That aunt of hers was a psycho to match, so I bailed."

"That sounds familiar."

"Yeah. I know," he said. "But... you were never childish. You just got caught up in stuff that *did* matter."

Grace didn't say anything at first and then she looked at him.

"You said some things," she said.

"You did too," he said.

"Fair."

Stefano leaned forward with his elbows on his knees.

"I was mad," he said. "And confused. And I believed things that weren't true. I let people tell me who you were instead of asking you."

"And I let anger talk for me. I wasn't thinking straight."

"I heard about everything," Stefano said. "Clarita wrote me."

Grace smiled at that.

"You know she ran that place?" Grace leaned sideways and asked in shock.

"She runs everywhere," Stefano said. "Even from a cell."

The pair of them laughed again and Stefano grabbed a cupcake from the box.

"You ever forgive me?" Grace asked.

"Yeah," he said. "I forgave you before you even got locked up. I was just dragging it out."

They sat in the sun and Grace finished another cupcake and handed him another one too.

"So, no hard feelings?" she asked.

"None," he said.

Later that week, Grace went to the studio. It wasn't big. In fact, it looked like it was just a basement with soundproof foam on the walls. Her old friend Niko's brother still worked there and he let her book a few hours for free.

"You ready?" he asked.

"Let's find out," Grace said.

She sang her songs — the new ones about broken trust and shame. She sang the ones about faith and choosing grace. She didn't expect anyone to listen, but she needed to sing them. She decided to post them online but she didn't promote them. She just uploaded and logged off. But two weeks later, one song started to get shared. Then another. She got a message from a girl in Ohio. Then one from a boy in London. They all said the same thing. *Your song helped me.*

Grace smiled.

She didn't go back to *Amor en la Cabina*. She didn't go back to the salon either. Brooke sent her a message though and said she heard the songs and was proud. Grace hadn't replied.

Grace walked through town one afternoon and ran into Stefano. He was coming out of a coffee shop. He froze when he saw her.

That night, she lit a candle and sat on her bed with her Bible open. Clarita used to say that grace wasn't something you earned. It was something you gave to others and to yourself. Grace touched the pages and whispered, "Thank you."

She wasn't sure who she was thankful to but she had never felt this grateful for just being alive before. Then, she picked up her pen and started to write again. There was something different about her now.

Something about Grace...

**

"For it is by grace you have been saved, through faith—and this is not from yourselves, it is the gift of God— not by works, so that no one can boast."

~ Ephesians 2:8-9 NIV

www.ingramcontent.com/pod-product-compliance
Lightning Source LLC
Chambersburg PA
CBHW031209260626
47169CB00004B/1293